A Hotwife's Filthy Wish

Wife Sharing With Friends

Lacey Cross

Twisted Rose Publishing

Contents

Chapter 1

Breathing in deeply, I try to relax as I settle into the lounge chair by the resort pool in Cabo San Lucas. The scent of chlorine masks the smell of the ocean just steps from the edge of the resort. I've always liked the smell of chlorine, so it's not unpleasant. My husband, Joey, stretches out in the chair next to me, and it's nice to see him unwinding from his stressful job as an accountant.

He's been teasing me and working me up for this trip to Cabo for weeks because he arranged for me to have some sexy fun with another guy while we're here. I bought a gorgeous purple lingerie set for the trip, and I've yet to use it. The plan is to wear it one of these nights to thrill him.

A couple of months ago at his work's Christmas party, I played the part of Santa's helper to pass out gifts and ended up fucking the guy from his work who was dressed up like Santa.

Caleb made one sexy Santa, and as his helper, I helped myself to his cock during the party while Joey watched.

Eventually Joey couldn't resist temptation, and he came over to fuck my mouth. Being spit roasted between the man I love and a massive cock in my pussy was an experience I won't forget.

As a Christmas present to all the employees, his work planned an all-expense paid trip to Cabo for a week in February. Joey has it all arranged that I'll get an evening with Caleb while we're here, but Joey's being mysterious about when it will happen.

We've been in Cabo for two days, and I've yet to get Caleb's cock in me. Whenever I pester Joey about it, all he says is, "Soon." Yeah, well *soon* my dear husband is going to have a sexually crazed wife on his hands. Wait, who am I kidding? He already has a sexually crazed wife. I love vacation sex, and knowing I get to fuck Caleb again makes me even hornier.

The resort where his company booked our rooms is gorgeous. We're staying for six nights, and each day the company has an event planned for everyone. Yesterday, we went sailing along the coast on a sunset cruise. Tonight, there's a banquet at the resort, along with a speech from the president of the company and then a presentation. The office voted for various humorous awards to give out to their coworkers, so it's supposed to be a lighthearted couple of hours. Joey is looking forward to it more than I am, but so far, the resort is treating us like royalty, so the food is bound to be delicious. I'm interested in going just for that.

I've seen Caleb several times so far on the trip, but we've only said hello and briefly chatted. He didn't bring anyone, which makes me feel better. I'm not interested in fucking a guy who has a girlfriend unless it's an open relationship. This isn't the first time I've seen him since the Christmas party. Joey invited him over to our house a few weeks later, and he fucked me on the coffee table.

Knowing that Joey arranged a play date with Caleb in Cabo has turned me into a nympho. Joey and I have already had sex four times since we got here. Even though we were exhausted from traveling, I jumped him as soon as we got into the hotel room, and with the way my pussy is buzzing just from lying here in the sun, I'm planning on fucking him before the banquet tonight.

Besides Caleb, another coworker — a guy named Ben — keeps drawing my attention. He's a super sexy older guy with streaks of gray in his hair and mature laugh lines on his face. I've caught his eye twice, and the twinkle in them makes me think he's fun loving.

The company allowed everyone to bring one person with them, and when I saw Ben with a woman who looked to be in her early 20s, I joked with Joey that his coworker likes them young. He laughed and said that Ben's single and that was his daughter. It pleased me to know he's single. I mean, not that I'm planning on fucking him or anything, but it gives me free license to imagine a three-some with him and Caleb whenever I see one of them. I'm horny and having fun with my slutty fantasies so far on this trip.

I shift positions on the lounge chair to avoid squirming. It's warm under the sun, but it's more than just the outside temperature heating me up. The pool's sparking blue water is gorgeous, and the palm trees lining the pool area are beautiful. We came to the pool to relax, but how am I supposed to unwind when I'm surrounded by smoking-hot men in swim shorts or Speedos?

Joey's squeeze to my hand brings me back to the present.

"Baby, do you want to swim some more, or should we head back to the room until dinner?"

A flame of desire kindles between my thighs. Oh yeah, the room sounds like a perfect plan. I give him my best sultry smile.

"I think there's some pressing business we need to attend to in our room."

He mock groans. "Didn't you get enough of me this morning?"

The memory of our earlier quickie is still fresh in my mind, and my pussy throbs. I purr, "I could never get enough of you. I've been thinking of your cock all day, and I need you inside me."

We just won't mention I've also been thinking of every cock that walks past.

Joey chuckles. "You're such a little slut sometimes."

I stand up and tug on his hand. "You love it when I'm a slut for *you*."

When he gets up, he pulls me into his arms for a deep kiss. "Yeah, you're my slut, and don't you forget it."

Lust blossoms in my stomach. I love it when he gets possessive.

I nod. "Only yours."

We link hands and make our way to the hotel lobby. I swear to God Joey is taking his time. I try to walk faster, but he keeps a firm grip on my hand and makes me slow down. When he stops to chat with a couple of people, I want to pout, but I have to play nice. Plus, it's not like I haven't gotten plenty of sex so far. I suppose I can wait a few more minutes.

By the time we get to our room, lust is burning in my brain and all I can think about is fucking him. As soon as the door shuts, I pounce. I shove him onto the bed, and he falls onto his back, laughing. "Whoa, okay...I guess you can have my cock if you insist."

I grin wickedly. "Oh, I insist all right. Get it out."

Making quick work of my bikini bottoms, I shimmy them down my hips and then remove my bikini top. Joey pulls his shorts down, but he's not moving fast enough for me. When he gets them down to his knees, I yank them off the rest of the way and flick them over my shoulder. They hit the wall before falling to the floor.

Joey's cock is already hard, so he must have been thinking about this on our way upstairs. I lick my lips and crawl toward him, rubbing my body against his. "Do you want me on top?"

"Hell yes!" He grabs my hips as I straddle him and lower myself onto his shaft. This is going to be fast, just like our quickie this morning, but I'm too horny to care about prolonging the pleasure. As I sink down on him, I rub my clit and moan. This is just what the doctor ordered.

"Fuck, you're so wet," he growls, grabbing my ass and pulling me harder down on him.

Resting one hand on his chest, I continue to rub my clit as I bob up and down on his lap. I moan loudly as he thrusts his hips upwards, loving the way he fills me. Delight runs up and down my body as I rock on his shaft. Since I'm feeling in control today, I chant, "Come for me," as I ride him faster and faster.

He thrashes under me as if he's trying to hold back, and once his eyes roll to the back of his head, I know I've won. When he groans in release, I come with him. Fireworks explode along the corner of my vision as my pussy clenches around his cock. I fuck him through the waves of pleasure as he unloads inside me for the second time today.

When my orgasm subsides, I lean my forehead against his neck and try to catch my breath.

"Oh god, you're going to be the death of me," he pants.

I giggle. "Yeah, but what a way to go."

Within moments, I'm next to him and we're snuggled together. I'm so relaxed I might just melt into the bed. I idly scan the room, and I study the plush chair facing the corner of the bed.

I tap him on his belly and giggle as I gesture in the chair's direction. "Don't you think that chair would be the perfect spot to sit while you watch Caleb fuck me?"

"Huh, maybe."

He's non-committal, as if he hadn't ever considered it. Maybe, my ass. I can tell he's having fun keeping me on tenterhooks about his plans. That's probably exactly where he's going to sit while I get railed by Caleb's massive cock.

I don't press him any further, and when he and I both yawn, I let my thoughts float away. A nap before the banquet is sounding good.

CHAPTER 2

Dinner was delicious, just as I expected. The awards ceremony is over, but the party's still going. It's turned into an impromptu comedy hour while Joey's coworkers take the microphone and tell funny work stories. People are laughing and having a good time, but I don't understand some jokes since I don't know the technical side of Joey's job as an accountant. But the atmosphere is pleasant, so I'm not racing to get out of here.

I wore a sapphire-blue silk dress that leaves my shoulders bare and ends above the knees. Joey's hand has been resting on my thigh for the last five minutes, and he's been slowly inching it upwards. When he slides it more towards my inner thigh, it tickles, and I try to clench my knees together so I don't laugh.

Leaning towards him, I whisper in his ear. "You're being a naughty boy."

He turns towards me with a grin but keeps on inching his hand up my leg. My panties grow wet, and I want to shift so he can rub my pussy, but his coworkers might notice that. Ben, the hot older coworker, takes the microphone, and I'm momentarily distracted from Joey's fingers. Damn, Ben really is hot. Tonight's dress code is semiformal, and the way his shirt hugs his shoulders, I bet he's muscular and fit under his clothes.

Joey tries to get my attention. "Hey, Miri?"

I'm still admiring Ben and preoccupied. "Hmmm?"

Joey's voice is low, and he's close enough to my ear that no one else at the table could hear him. "If I gave you one wish to do whatever you wanted tonight, what would it be?"

What's this? Joey finally has my full attention. "One wish?"

He nods. "What is your heart's filthiest desire?"

The crowd laughs, and I look again at Ben telling his joke. Oh yeah, I know what my wish would be. I turn and kiss Joey softly before speaking.

"If I had one wish and could do whatever I wanted, I'd want to fuck Caleb and Ben tonight."

Joey's eyes widen like he's surprised. "Ben?"

I don't want him to know exactly how hot I find Ben, so I shrug. "Yeah, I mean he's got that sexy older guy vibe, and he seems nice."

Yeah, he seems like he'd be nice to fuck and probably knows a thing or two about pleasuring a woman, given his age.

I think of something else. "Oh, and..." A blush creeps up my face. This next part is hard to admit.

"Yes?"

I try to not be embarrassed. This is my husband, for Christ's sake. I should be able to tell him about my dirtiest fantasies.

"I'd want them to treat me like a sex doll, like I'm just a hole they're using."

Oh, God. I said it. My filthiest desire. Um, shit, I hope no one else heard that. I glance around the table, and none of the other couples are paying attention to us.

"Huh." Joey takes my hand and kisses the back of it. "Guess I better go see if Caleb minds having company tonight."

What? I don't have time to question him, because he drops my hand and heads towards the back of the room. My entire body buzzes, and I can't concentrate on anything being said. All I can think about is how Joey is off asking Caleb if he's willing to share me.

Tonight! The jerk didn't tell me we had plans with Caleb tonight. He was obviously going to just spring it on me.

Ben passes the microphone to someone else, and I don't pay attention to the next person who takes it. When Caleb slides into Joey's vacant seat, heat rushes between my legs and I'm flustered.

His voice is deep. "I hear you want to fuck two guys."

My mouth forms an 'O', and I take a moment to speak. "Um, is that okay?"

He laughs. "Oh yeah, sounds like fun."

Shit, is anyone listening to this? I peer around the table and everyone is focused on the speaker. Thank God.

His hand brushes against my knee, and I almost jump while another splash of wetness hits my panties. Jesus, now he's teasing me too. Caleb caresses my leg while pretending to pay attention to the last couple of speakers. He gets tantalizingly close to the edge of my panties and then moves his hand away again. I'm a vibrating bundle of energy, and my need for him blots out everything else.

When the party breaks up, I'm so keyed up I'm about ready to throw myself on Caleb's cock. Joey and Ben walk up to us before I do something stupid in front of all their coworkers.

Joey's gaze sweeps over me speculatively before he grins. "Hey, let's get out of here."

I shiver from arousal and rise from my seat. "Yes, please."

Joey takes my hand. Caleb and Ben tail behind us as we leave the room.

"Where are we going?" I ask him quietly.

His voice is low, matching my volume. "Our room. I hear it's got a chair that gives a good view of people fucking on the bed."

Ohhh, hell yeah. My pussy clenches, and I want to skip to the elevator.

CHAPTER 3

In the elevator, I drop Joey's hand, and the doors are barely closed before Caleb presses me against the wall and ravishes my mouth. Well, hello there. Between kisses, he groans, "I want to fuck you right here."

I get a nice zing of lust at his words. It's been less than two months since his cock was inside me, but it feels like an eternity. I've been thinking about this trip and hoping nothing would mess up my chance to fuck him again.

Sliding my arms around Caleb's neck, I meet his passion with my own. Joey and Ben lean against the opposite wall so they can watch the Caleb and Miri Elevator Show. I bet it's a good show.

Caleb continues to kiss me as he slides his hand between my legs. When he brushes his fingers against the silk of my panties, the friction against the smooth fabric makes my pussy tingle. I buck my hips, needing more. My reaction encourages him to push past the elastic band and slide two fingers inside me. I moan into Caleb's mouth as he massages the perfect spot against my cave wall.

Caleb breaks off the kiss and murmurs in my ear. "Do you want us to fuck you?" His hot breath tickles the sensitive skin under my earlobe, and I bite my lip to hold in more moans.

When I don't answer, he asks again. "Do you, Miri? Do you want Ben's cock...and my cock...both inside you...using you?"

His words make my legs quiver. I nod and whimper. I'm so fucking turned on right now, he could take me here in the elevator if he wanted. All three of them could take turns using my holes, and I'd just beg for more.

Caleb steps back and flips me around, shoving my breasts against the cool steel of the elevator wall. *Ohhh, this is good.* He doesn't ask for permission or give me time to say no, which is *exactly* what I want tonight.

He pulls my panties down to my knees and then pins my shoulder against the wall as he slides his fingers inside me again. He finger fucks me roughly, and I gasp as I lean into his touch. Pings of delight ripple through me as he works my cunt. I wasn't expecting him to be all over me in the elevator, but this is fabulous.

He removes his hands from my shoulder and pussy, grabs my ass, and pulls my hips back, forcing me to bend over. I have to place my palms flat against the wall to steady myself as he grinds his hardness against my ass. God, I need his cock inside me. The fabric of his trousers is thin enough that I can feel the ridge of his cock, but all he's doing is smearing my wetness over the front of him and making me even more desperate.

The elevator slows to a stop, and he lets go of my hips. I assume we're at our floor, but he quickly stands in front of me, blocking the view from the hallway as the door slides open. Shit, maybe not? I stand up and adjust my dress back in order when someone from the hallway speaks.

"Oh, sorry, we're going down. Not up."

Ohhh, fuck. Yeah, this isn't our floor. My panties are still at my knees, and I flush from the embarrassment as I peek over Caleb's shoulder. An elderly couple smiles at us. Oh no, did they see anything?

Joey laughs. "No worries. You have a good night," and the door slides closed again.

Caleb turns around and smiles. "That was a close one."

I laugh nervously. "Yeah, it was. They almost got a surprise."

His eyes darken, and he kisses me again. Our tongues twine together and I mold myself against his body until the elevator reaches our floor.

We stumble out, and I almost feel as if I'm drunk as the four of us briskly stride towards the hotel room. Thank God the hallway is empty. We're walking like people on a mission.

Once inside our room, Joey takes over. "I want you guys to fuck her on the bed. I'll watch from the chair."

He motions towards the chair I was laughing about earlier. It really is in the perfect position to watch the action on the bed. He sits down and starts loosening his dress shirt as I kick off my high heels and yank my dress over my head. Having a threesome while Joey watches is going to be fucking amazing. My pussy desperately wants Caleb's cock inside her, so I'm not wasting time.

Caleb and Ben both start undressing as well, and I pause before removing my bra and panties so I can watch them. I already know what Caleb looks like naked, but I'm dying to see if Ben is as sexy under his clothes as I imagined he would be.

Ben's bulge is impressive, and when his pants hit the floor, his cock looks even larger. He's wearing boxer briefs, and they clearly outline his cock. I'm not sure I've ever seen a cock that size. Um, will it even fit?

My brain blips out for a moment when I realize I'm about to get fucked by two massive cocks. Caleb is very large, and now Ben is even bigger than Caleb. Holy fuck.

Joey whistles at Ben's cock. "Damn, you're going to ruin her with that thing."

I can tell by the gleeful tone of his voice that he really wants to watch me get ruined. How did I get so fucking lucky? My husband sees a dude with an enormous cock, and he's all excited for me to get pounded with it? I seriously have the best husband on the planet.

Caleb and Ben laugh at his words, and Ben says, "I aim to please."

Joey leans back in his chair and uses one hand to stroke his cock through his pants while gesturing towards me with his other hand. "Have at it. I want to hear my toy scream when she comes."

Ohhh fuck, that's hot. When I told Joey earlier that I wanted to be treated like a sex doll, I didn't think he would do or say anything to push me towards feeling that way. But him acting like I'm his toy to share and telling two guys to fuck me puts me in the frame of mind I craved.

Yep, it's time for this toy to get used.

As I reach behind me to unhook my bra, Joey and Caleb remove the rest of their clothes. My bra falls to the floor with barely a whisper as I step out of my panties.

It's odd to be naked in front of two guys I barely know, but I try not to focus on that. I'm a sexy goddess who is about to get her filthiest wish fulfilled. Goddesses don't have time to feel vulnerable and awkward when the action is about to start.

Putting an extra swing into my hips, I stroll over to Caleb and tip my head up towards him. He kisses me passionately and runs his hands over my body. The warmth of his palms sends a pleasant tingle to my pussy. Mmm, I always love how large his hands are and how he knows when to take charge with them. He threads his fingers through my hair, and I gasp as he tugs, forcing my head to tip back.

"Are you ready to get fucked mindless?" The slight growl in his voice gives me goosebumps.

"Yes, please. I need it."

Caleb chuckles and looks at Ben. "What do you think? Should we give her what she wants?"

Ben nods. "Let's do it. I heard she's begging to feel used."

Mmm, yes I am.

Ben continues. "Not that I blame her, since her husband is a bit of a softie. I bet he only fucks romantically, nice and slow."

Um... My breath catches from shock, and my eyes widen. My heart races as I glance towards Joey. What the hell is going on here?

Caleb laughs harshly. "I bet that's true."

Joey speeds up the rubbing of his cock through his pants and groans before he laughs along with them. "Oh, fuck off you two. Shut up and get on with it."

Ben grins and moves to stand next to Caleb. "I think we need to do a hole inspection first. See if we even want to fuck her."

Caleb nods. "Good idea."

I'm not exactly sure what a hole inspection includes, but the fire in my stomach tells me I don't care as long as I get something in one of those holes soon.

Caleb grips my shoulder and spins me until I'm facing the bed. Ben grabs my wrists as Caleb pushes my shoulder down to the mattress. Raw, wild need pulses through my pussy. I love being manhandled like this.

I bend over, and Caleb pulls my legs apart, forcing me to widen my stance. My face smashes against the comforter while Ben keeps hold of my wrists. Did they fucking choreograph this? Hell, maybe they've done this together more than once.

Ben says, "You check her pussy. I'm checking her ass."

Ohhhh, fuck.

"Wait," Joey calls out. "Use lube, so you can inspect it easier."

I hear the dresser opening before it slides closed again, and I tense in anticipation of what is about to happen.

"Good thinking," Ben replies, letting go of my wrists.

When my hands are free, I move them close to my face and grip the comforter. The squeeze of the lube bottle is loud, and drops of cold liquid rain onto my ass cheeks. Um, I think he missed the spot he was aiming for. I keep silent though since sex dolls don't talk.

Fingers explore along the length of my pussy lips. I assume it's Caleb, and a glance over my shoulder confirms it. He gathers moisture from my pussy and rubs circles around my clit. Holy fuck. I thought the guys were going to come in here and start fucking me immediately, but this is dirtier.

I straighten my head and stare unseeingly at the wall as Caleb continues his exploration of my pussy. His swirling fingers spread me wide as his thumb sinks into my ready wetness. Ben massages the lube into the crack of my ass, and I welcome his touch.

"Miri, spread your legs wider for me."

I obey, moving my feet even further apart. They are both standing close enough that I can feel the heat of their bodies, and Caleb's hard cock brushes against my thigh.

Caleb's "Good girl" makes me want to please them even more.

I tilt my head back and close my eyes, letting the sensations become my only focus. When Ben's lubed-up finger works its way into my ass, I groan involuntarily. He presses deeper as I squirm, and I suck in air, trying to hold in any further sounds. The quieter I am, the nastier this is.

Ben whistles softly. "That's a nice tight ass. I bet it'll feel good around my big fat cock."

"Yeah, I'm sure it will," Caleb murmurs. "You can stretch her ass out. I'm all about this wet pussy."

Uh...he thinks he's fucking me in the ass with that third leg he's sporting? A forbidden longing zings straight to my core, and I almost come all over Caleb's fingers. I squeeze my eyes shut, and I'm panting as I fight for control.

Holy fuck. Will he fuck my ass while Caleb is in my pussy? My entire body zings alive at the thought of being double stuffed.

Jesus, why didn't I think of this earlier? All day, I've been fantasizing about getting fucked by two men and somehow didn't consider it happening at the same time. To have the chance to do it with my husband watching is overwhelming, but this is an experience I'd want to share with him.

Ben laughs. "She has two tight holes to fill. Why not?"

Caleb's cock brushes against me again as both guys work their fingers inside me. Pleasure builds in my core, and I bite my lip and clutch the comforter tightly as my legs begin to shake.

Chapter 4

With sudden clarity, I know I really *do* want that monster inside my ass. This is the filthy wish I didn't know I lusted after. I won't be satisfied tonight unless I'm stuffed and stretched more than I've ever been.

"This hole is ready," Caleb announces, and his cock throbs against my thigh.

Ben slaps my ass. "I'm almost done getting this one ready. I need it to be loose and relaxed."

Ben continues to massage the lube around my asshole, and I whimper when he adds a second finger to the first one and presses them into my ass. They're treating me like I'm just holes to use, and it's exactly what I wanted. This is fucking amazing. Joey deserves a goddamn medal for arranging this.

Caleb runs the tip of his cock up and down the back of my leg. "I can't wait any longer. I need to fuck something."

I whimper as Ben removes his fingers and Caleb climbs onto the bed and lies down on his back.

"Climb up onto me and ride me like the cock-addicted slut you are."

This is the third time I've had sex with Caleb, and it's making the dirty talk even better because I've seen the softer side of him. I know he's not a jackass who means what he's saying.

And he's right; I am a cock-addicted slut. I'll do anything he wants tonight.

I nod eagerly, shift up onto the bed, and straddle him. He grips his cock to hold it steady, and I pause right before pressing down. I look over my shoulder at Joey and smile at him. "Is this a good view, my love?"

His cock is out of his pants, and he's stroking it slowly. He's nice and hard, and I bet he's leaking pre-cum. Mmmm...I know exactly how he tastes, and I wish he was in my mouth. The haze of lust in his eyes tells me he's been enjoying everything.

He has to clear his throat before he can talk. "Yes, it's a lovely view, but sex dolls can't speak. They just take cock."

My lips part slightly in surprise as Caleb holds onto my hips and thrusts up.

"Ohhh." I accidentally let a moan slip out as I sink onto his shaft. His wonderfully thick cock burrows its way to my core, and the pleasure almost short circuits my brain. Even though I've fucked him before, his size still surprises me. He's so thick it feels like he's splitting me apart. I rock my hips, enjoying how he massages every inch of my cave walls. He reaches up to play with my nipples, and spikes of bliss head straight to my clit. Mmmm, this is perfect.

He digs his fingers into my hips, dragging me up and down his shaft, and little sighs and peeps of pleasure escape me as I speed up my movements. I'm rushing towards an orgasm, and I don't want to stop.

"Kiss me," he demands, and I lean forward and plaster my lips against his.

I'm a woman possessed as my tongue tangles with his. He wraps his arms around me, and the blistering kiss sets my soul on fire. I'm so focused on the building desire in my core that I don't pay attention to anything else until I feel the tip of Ben's cock against my asshole.

I squeal into Caleb's mouth and grind harder against his shaft. Oh god, this is why they have me in this position. Caleb is lying on the bed at the perfect angle for Joey to see both their cocks sliding into me from his chair.

"Take it slow," Joey warns. "She isn't used to having such a gigantic cock in her ass. I don't want my toy hurt."

My head spins, and I have the insane urge to laugh and moan at the same time. Joey taking care of me in a filthy way is exactly like something he would do. Such a romantic.

Caleb continues to kiss me as Ben applies more lube to my ass. Even with the added slickness, I know it's going to hurt when he presses in, but the initial discomfort never lasts long.

"Get ready." Ben gives the warning a few moments before the pressure against my opening increases.

I try to relax, knowing it will hurt less, but it doesn't stop the pain.

"Fuuuuuuck," I cry out as he pushes inside slowly.

Oh god, he's so fucking huge. I thought Caleb was splitting me in two, but this is beyond anything I could have imagined. Pain shoots through me, twisted with intense pleasure. It's a delicious thrill as he stretches my ass.

Caleb continues to piston his hips up, thrusting into my pussy while Ben sinks deeper inside me. I whimper as pings of bliss explode in my mind.

I hope Joey can see everything. Thinking back on what happened at the work Christmas party, I can't help but wish Joey would come fuck my mouth like he did then. I could have all my holes filled for real. Shit, I want that.

I'm distracted from my thoughts when Ben pauses. I can tell he's in my ass as far as he can go because he pulls out and presses back in. The pain is gone, and it's replaced by a rapture I've never felt before.

As both guys fuck me, I lose my mind and can't keep quiet any longer. I'm writhing and moaning continuously as they use both my holes.

"Fuck, this feels soooo good," Caleb murmurs, as he squeezes my breasts and tugs on my nipples.

Ben's voice is strained when he agrees. "Yeah, I could use this piece of ass all night long."

Caleb grunts and thrusts faster. "I think Joey's toy likes being used."

"God yes," I moan, as every press from Ben makes me take Caleb's cock further inside me. "Use me."

Caleb laughs harshly. "We're not stopping until we're done with you."

I grind against Caleb's cock and speed up my rhythm, thinking of nothing else except the growing bliss. The bed creaks from our combined movements, and my tiny mewling joins in with wet slapping sounds and the moans and groans from the guys. It's all too much, and my body shakes as I rush towards my orgasm.

Both cocks massaging my insides create a ripple of pleasure through me. My cries of "Oh god" turn into whimpers and moans as Ben pushes me down closer to Caleb so he can put his foot on the bed and drill into my ass.

I bite down on Caleb's shoulder as I explode with pleasure. My pussy clenches down hard, and I scream as I come. Energy courses all the way from my fingers to my toes as the guys fuck me through my orgasm.

I collapse on top of Caleb, but the guys don't stop using me. My pussy flutters with aftershocks of pleasure. The bliss is too much, and my brain switches off. I become a mindless fucktoy that they both continue to use, and time holds no meaning.

Ben comes first. He roars and fills my ass with his hot cum a few seconds before Caleb blows his load into my pussy. They fuck their cum back into me for a few strokes before pulling out.

Ben groans, "God, that was amazing," as I roll off of Caleb onto my back.

I close my eyes and drift while one of them goes into the bathroom. I'm surprised when hands hook around my thighs and tug me to the end of the bed. What's going on?

Someone pushes my legs open, and I look down at Caleb kneeling between them. He puts my knees on his shoulders while he leans in to lick me. He spreads my labia, pushing his tongue into my dripping slit as he cleans up from the mess he made in my pussy.

"Ohhh," I moan, and my hips move with his rhythm.

I twist the comforter in my hands as each swipe of his tongue pings me with gentle pleasure. I've never had anyone clean me up like this before, and it's the right kind of dirty.

Just when I'm about to come again, Ben speaks up from the bathroom doorway. "It's my turn."

Caleb and Ben switch places, and Ben's mouth latches onto my clit. He sucks and swirls his tongue around my swollen nub, and I moan loudly, which makes him pause his licking.

I tilt my hips, desperate for his tongue. "Oh god, don't stop!"

Ben slides his hands up the outside of my thighs and cups my ass. He squeezes my cheeks as he attacks my clit again. I buck towards his face and peep out tiny moans as the ecstasy builds.

"You sound so damn sexy," he murmurs with passion.

His tongue drives me crazy, and I can't focus on anything but the pleasure. I press my pussy against his face, desperate for another orgasm.

I almost don't notice when Caleb kneels on the bed next to my face. His cock is hard again, and he's stroking it as he moves it towards my mouth. Ohhh fuck, this is filthy. Caleb presses the head against my lips, and I open as wide as I can so he can slide in. I suck greedily on the tip, enjoying the combined flavor of our juices.

"Fuck, she tastes so good," Ben says as he slides his fingers into my pussy and fucks me with them while he continues to suck on my clit.

I moan around Caleb's cock and wrap my hand around his shaft so I can stroke him while he fucks my mouth.

Ben stops licking me and announces, "Fuck it."

He holds my legs and stands up. I barely have time to wonder what he's doing before my feet are on his shoulders and he's sliding his cock into my pussy. Since he's thicker than Caleb, his cock stretches my pussy even further than it was earlier. I'm immediately on the edge of my orgasm.

Caleb pumps into my mouth slowly while Ben sets a punishing pace. My body responds to each movement, and I whimper and moan with each deep thrust. I can't take much more of this, and I'm going to come any second.

"Be a good girl and come for me," Ben commands with an extra hard thrust that shoots me over the edge.

My body convulses with pleasure, and Caleb's cock muffles my scream. My orgasm seems never-ending as Ben hammers into me. He doesn't let up until he groans and shudders as he blows a second massive load deep into my pussy.

Ben coming lights a fire in Caleb, and his thrusts become shorter and quicker. Within moments, a burst of cum hits the back of my throat as several more spurts coat my tongue. I try to swallow and clean him up the best I can, but saliva and cum run out of my mouth when he pulls out.

He leans over and kisses me softly, sucking his cum off my tongue. Jesus, Caleb is one dirty mofo. It's awesome.

I wonder if Joey would ever let me fuck Caleb again. The same guy three times seems a bit more than a casual fuck, but I can't help but want it. Sure, Ben's also got a great cock, but something about Caleb's ability to fuck me hard and yet be sweet makes him a perfect fuck buddy.

A warm fuzziness steals over me as Caleb pulls me up onto the bed so I'm not hanging off it. My eyes drift closed. I'm on a higher plane of existence, one where nothing matters but the amazing afterglow of having two massive cocks double penetrating me and using me.

The guys talk quietly, and I don't follow the conversation. I listen to the sound of clothes rustling, and I assume they're getting dressed. The bed dips next to my head, and I open my eyes when a hand strokes my cheek.

Caleb is fully clothed and looking at me with a soft smile. "Thank you for another wonderful night. Joey is one lucky man."

Joey's "I am" pleases me.

"Thank you, Caleb…" I don't know how close Ben is, so I raise my voice. "And you too, Ben. This was wonderful."

Ben laughs. "Believe me, the pleasure was all mine."

I smile in his general direction and close my eyes again and doze while Caleb and Ben leave. Within minutes, the room is silent.

Chapter 5

Joey climbs on the bed next to me and kisses me gently. "You're such a beautiful mess."

I peek at him and search his eyes to make sure he really means it. The love shining from him warms me. He cuddles close, but I can't fully relax because I expect him to pounce on me any moment. The last two times I fucked someone else, he was all over me as soon as we were alone. He rubs my arm and tries nothing further. Huh, maybe he came while watching me get double stuffed.

Wetness drips out of me, and since he's not seeming like he wants to fuck me, I tease him. "I *am* a mess. I need a shower."

"You do. I'll go start the water for you."

He kisses my nose and climbs off the bed. When I hear the shower running, I get up and dig out a cotton nightgown from the dresser. I finger the new purple lace lingerie set before closing the drawer. I'll wear that for him tomorrow.

"Your shower awaits, my lady."

Joey's standing in the bathroom's doorway, and I stand on my tiptoes to brush my lips against his as I pass.

"Why thank you, my kind sir."

I leave the bathroom door open. When I step into the shower, the water is the perfect temperature. My wonderful husband knows exactly what I like.

I stand under the spray for a bit, doing nothing but letting the water cascade over me. My pussy and ass aren't sore yet, but I can tell they will be by morning. A person can't get pounded in both holes by two huge cocks and not expect a little tenderness.

Squeezing body wash out of its travel container, I lather up a washcloth and run it over my body, washing off the cum on my inner thighs and butt. Movement outside of the frosted glass shower door tells me Joey is in the bathroom.

He's naked, and he leans against the counter while he watches me. A simmer of desire coils in my stomach. I really need him to fuck me to show me what happened tonight doesn't change anything between us.

"Want to join me?" I use my cutest sing-song tone in the hopes to entice him.

His voice is lust-thickened when he says, "No, I'm just enjoying the show."

Heh, he definitely enjoys watching me. When I'm rinsing off, I spend extra time with my hand between my legs, pretending I'm doing a very thorough cleaning. I purposely face him so he can see where my hand is.

After a minute of touching myself, his voice is stern. "I think you're clean enough."

I hold in a giggle. "I think you're right."

Turning off the shower, I step out, and he immediately wraps a towel around me and dries me off. All I have to do is stand there as he bends down and starts at my feet and works his way up. I widen my legs as he gets closer to my pussy so he's able to rub the cotton against me. I give a soft moan as he spends extra time between my legs, and when the towel drops away, he uses his fingers to rub along my folds instead.

I run my fingers through his hair, and he leans in to kiss along the soft curls of my landing strip. Maybe I was wrong about him not wanting more tonight, or it's possible I got him worked up while he was watching me shower. My pussy is loving the attention, so it doesn't matter why.

He uses his hands to pull open my pussy lips, and he presses his face against me so he can massage my clit with his tongue.

"Ohhh, god," I moan and tilt my hips towards his face to give him better access.

The room spins a little, and my knees go weak as he licks and sucks the sensitive bundle of nerves. I'm not in any danger of falling, but I'm feeling unsteady as pleasure runs up and down the length of my body.

He slips a finger inside me, and I buck against him and cry out from the pleasure. While I'm not one to normally stop my husband from giving me a thrilling tongue bath, I really need him to fill me up with his cum. Ending the night with a pussy full of his seed is my favorite part of being a hotwife. No matter how slutty I am, I want Joey to be the last guy to come inside me.

I tug on his hair, forcing him to look up at me. "Love, I need you to fuck me. Please?"

He stands and holds my hand as we move to the bed. Before we lie down, he pulls me against him for a deep kiss. His hard cock pokes against my stomach, so I reach between us and stroke him while our tongues swirl together.

I'm so in love with him. My heart feels like it's ready to burst. I'm having a wonderful time being a hotwife, and it's so fucking hot to see how turned on he gets watching me with other men, but I'd give it all up if he asked me to. All the enormous cocks in the world can't compare to this moment with him right here, right now. His cock is the only one that really matters to me.

He gives a sharp intake of breath when I slide my hand lower and run my fingers over his balls before moving back to the tip. He's already leaking pre-cum, and I swirl my fingers around the head of his cock.

He groans. "No more teasing. I need you."

I let go of his cock and give him a sassy, "As you wish, sir," before climbing onto the bed. I'm too tired to be on top again, so I lie down in the middle on my back. He joins me, and I open my legs to welcome him.

He settles between my thighs and rubs the head of his cock along my slit. Fuuuck, now he's the one teasing me. He takes his time and gets the tip of his cock nice and wet before pushing into me.

As he stretches me for the last time tonight, the pings of delight are stronger than what I felt earlier. This is how I know he's the one for me. It's just sex with the other men, but no matter how slutty I get with Joey, we're always making love.

"God, I love you," he groans as he begins to thrust.

I hold on to his shoulders and wrap my legs around him. He's being gentle, and I appreciate the care he's taking with me.

I feel so incredibly full and happy. "I love you too."

Keeping my eyes glued to his, I watch desire flicker over his face. His pleasure brings me closer to the edge, but I don't want to come yet. I'm waiting to come when he fills me.

"Please, faster," I beg.

"Yes, baby," he growls and picks up the pace.

He quickens his thrusts while still not fucking me hard. I'm so close to coming, and I can't wait any longer. I unwrap my legs from his waist and spread them wide as I put my feet down, pushing my hips up to meet him and force him deeper. He hits the perfect spot, and my eyes glaze as waves of pleasure crash over me.

"Ohhh, god!" I cry out as my climax builds and I splinter into a thousand pieces. I'm free-falling through space when he growls and unloads his warm cum deep inside me. He thrusts in a few more times, making sure I get every drop.

We're both flushed and panting when he climbs off me. Holy fuck, that was a perfect ending to the night. I float in a daze for a few moments, and when I come back to my senses, Joey is in his own little world as he lies on his back, staring at the ceiling.

Oh yeah, I think I fucked my dear husband senseless.

Curling against him, I wrap a leg around him and snuggle into the crook of his arm. I trace figure-eights on his chest, and I can tell the moment he can think again because he brings his hand up to rub my back.

I keep my tone light and flirty. "So, did you enjoy watching me get stuffed by two guys?"

He gives a strangled laugh. "Yeah, that was good."

Thinking about how wonderful having all my holes used reminds me of my thought in the middle of it all.

"You know, you could have used my mouth while the guys were inside me."

His hand stills for a moment. "You seemed a little busy."

Giving his shoulder a little kiss, I purr at him. "I would have gladly sucked your cock."

He rubs my back again but is quiet for a moment, as if he's thinking. "Guess I'll know that for next time."

A zing runs through me. Next time? Nah, he's just fucking with me.

I tease him back. "Yep, guess you'll have to do it next time."

He pulls me close and kisses the top of my head. I'm exhausted, but my brain churns at the thought of him in my mouth while two other guys fuck me. It's really too bad there isn't another work event planned. I smile softly at myself and force myself to relax.

Okay, yeah, I'm totally a slut. I guess I'll just have to think of another excuse to get double stuffed in the future.

The End

About Lacey Cross

I'm mainly a writer who got bored during the pandemic and turned to erotica out of desperation. I found out I love the creativity and challenge of self-publishing sexy stories. I write a variety of kinks, but most are wife sharing with a touch of BDSM power control.

Connect with me at:

https://lacey-cross.com/

Acknowledgments

I want to thank my wonderful editor, Wordcat. I hope I tell you often enough how lucky I am to have you as a friend!